Wishes Come True

Random House 🏠 New York

ISBN: 978-0-7364-2723-4

www.randomhouse.com/kids

MANUFACTURED IN SINGAPORE

10 9 8 7 6 5 4 3

Contents

Make-believe Bride . . . . Page 5

Hoppily Ever After . . . . Page 29

A Dazzling Day . . . . Page 53

THE LITTLE MERMAID

Make-believe Bride

By K. Emily Hutta • Illustrated by the Disney Storybook Artists

*A*riel's secret grotto was her favorite place in the whole undersea world—especially now that a statue of Prince Eric was there.

"Oh, Flounder, it's almost like having Eric with me!" Ariel said with a sigh.

"Ariel!" cried Sebastian. "Get ahold of yourself. That's nothing but a hunk of rock!"

Ariel placed her head on the statue's shoulder. "Why, yes, I'd love to marry you, Eric," she said, pretending.

"*Marry?*" Sebastian roared. "You will do no such thing. In the name of His Royal Majesty King Triton, I forbid this kind of talk."

"It's a statue, remember?" Ariel said. "I'm just playing make-believe."

"We can have the wedding right here in the grotto," Ariel continued. "You'll both help me, won't you?"

"Help you with what?" Sebastian asked as Ariel showered him with decorations. "It's make-believe. You said so yourself."

"Oh, dream weddings are every bit as much work as real weddings," Ariel said.

"I think Prince Eric is dressed perfectly for a wedding,"
Ariel said, looking lovingly at the statue. "But I'll need
something fancier to wear!"

"And, Flounder," Ariel said, "you may be the chef. I want you to prepare the most wonderful foods you can imagine."

"Seaweed gelatin . . . plankton pudding . . . ," Flounder suggested.

"And don't forget the wedding cake!" Ariel cried.

"Just leave it to me," Flounder said proudly. "This will be a wedding feast like no one has ever seen!"

"Oh, I can hardly wait!" Ariel exclaimed. "I can picture the entire ceremony. My sisters will make such beautiful bridesmaids. And my father will be so proud as we—"

"Your father?" Sebastian looked as if he was ready to faint.
"Oh, don't be such a party pooper, Sebastian," Ariel said
lightly. "Remember . . . it's all just pretend."

"I'm leaving," Sebastian said. "I can't take any more of this nonsense."

"Well, that's a shame," Ariel said to Flounder. "Who will conduct the wedding's grand orchestra?"

"Grand orchestra?" Sebastian asked, stopping in his tracks.

"Of course you're my first choice, Sebastian," Ariel said. "But—"

"*But* nothing!" Sebastian cried. "A crab must do what a crab must do! The show—er, rather, the wedding—must go on!" Grabbing a candlestick, Sebastian began to conduct his pretend orchestra.

"May I have this dance, Ariel?" Flounder asked, bowing politely.

"With pleasure, kind sir!" Ariel said, laughing as she and Flounder waltzed and twirled until they were both dizzy.

That evening, Ariel was trying on her veil when Flounder arrived with a beautiful string of pearls.

"They belong to a friend," Flounder said. "You can borrow them."

Now Ariel had something old (the dinglehopper to comb her hair), something new (her veil), something borrowed (the pearls), and something blue (her blue shell bracelet).

"That's everything a bride needs!" Ariel exclaimed.

The next morning, Sebastian scuttled after Ariel as she
swam from the palace.

"I hope no one sees us," Sebastian said nervously.
"It might be hard to explain where you're going dressed
like this!"

Flounder was waiting for them outside the grotto.

"Are you ready, Ariel?" Flounder asked. Ariel nodded, and Flounder escorted her into the grotto.

"Dum-dum-de-dum, dum-dum-de-dum . . . ," Sebastian sang the wedding march as his orchestra played. He stopped abruptly when Ariel passed by.

"Ohhhhhh," wailed Sebastian. "Weddings always make me cry!"

Sebastian cleared his throat importantly. "Do you, Princess Ariel, take this . . . er . . . statue to be your make-believe husband?"

"I do!" Ariel declared.

"And do you, Mr. Pretend Prince, take this princess to be your make-believe wife?" Sebastian went on.

"He says he does," Ariel said with a giggle.

"Well then, I pronounce you imaginary husband and wife," Sebastian said.

"Hooray!" Flounder cheered as Ariel tossed her bouquet.

Ariel hugged her friends. "Oh, thank you! This has been a wonderful dream wedding!" she cried. "And now I'm inviting you both to my *real* wedding to Prince Eric. I'm not sure when, or where, or how, but I know it *will* happen. Nothing can stand in the way of true love!"

"Nothing," Flounder agreed dreamily.

Ariel sighed with happiness, imagining a kiss from Prince Eric.

"Yikes!" she cried suddenly. She realized she was actually kissing a very startled Flounder!

"Aha!" Sebastian shouted. "See what comes of silly notions about marrying human princes! . . . As if that could ever really happen . . ."

DISNEY PRINCESS

THE PRINCESS AND THE FROG

Hoppily Ever After

Adapted by Elle D. Risco

Illustrated by Jean-Paul Orpiñas
and Scott Tilley

Designed by Tony Fejeran

As the sun rose over the bayou, Tiana was already hard at work. Just yesterday, she had been a *human* waitress. Today, thanks to a magic spell, she was a *frog*! Tiana had just finished building a raft that would get her and her lazy companion—the prince-turned-frog Naveen—back to New Orleans.

31

After she finished, Tiana began steering the raft down the
bayou. Naveen lounged in the back, strumming his ukulele.
    Suddenly, a huge alligator surfaced right next to them! The
two frogs huddled together in fear.

Luckily, the alligator was friendly! His name was Louis, and boy, did he love jazz! He even had his own trumpet!

Tiana rolled her eyes as Naveen started talking to Louis. There was no time to waste—they had to figure out how to become human again!

Louis had an idea. He told Tiana and Naveen that an old
woman named Mama Odie knew magic and could help them.
Louis agreed to take the two frogs to see her. So Tiana and
Naveen hopped on top of Louis and set off to find Mama Odie.

Just as things were starting to look up, a fly flew by. Tiana and Naveen tried to snag it with their tongues—and became hopelessly tangled in a knot!

Luckily, the fly flew back. He turned out to be a helpful firefly named Ray.

Ray managed to untangle Tiana
and Naveen. Then he offered to lead
them to Mama Odie.

Ray called his firefly family to light the way
through the misty bayou.

Tiana was beginning
to like Ray. He knew how
to get things done—unlike Naveen!
And Ray also had a soft side, which he
revealed when he started talking about his
true love. "My girl? That's Evangeline. She's
the prettiest firefly that ever did glow."

"Don't settle down too quickly, my friend," Naveen said to Ray.

Tiana was about to scold Naveen for being insensitive. But suddenly, he got caught by a frog hunter! Then Tiana was captured, too!

Louis didn't realize that Naveen had been captured, so he ran to hide in some pricker bushes. But brave Ray raced to the rescue! He went straight for one of the frog hunters and flew right up his nose! The startled hunter let go of his net, and Naveen hopped into the water.

When he came up for air, Naveen saw Tiana in a cage.
He couldn't let the frog hunters take her away!

Naveen used his tongue to latch on to the boat as if he were
a water-skier.

Tiana was shocked that the selfish prince was actually trying
to rescue her!

After Naveen climbed into the boat, he freed Tiana from the cage. Then they both started hopping all around. The hunters swatted and swung wildly, but they hit each other instead of the frogs!

Bruised and tired, the frog hunters collapsed in a heap at the bottom of their boat.

"These two are like no frogs I've ever seen!" one of them said. "They're smart!"

Tiana was grateful that Naveen had come back for her. She was starting to look at him in a new light.

While Ray pulled all the prickers out of Louis, Tiana
decided to put the time to good use and cook dinner.
"How about some swamp gumbo?" she asked.

Tiana asked Naveen to
mince some mushrooms, but he
wasn't sure how to even begin the simple job.
   "When you live in a castle, everything is done
for you," Naveen explained as he struggled.
"I don't know how to do anything."

Tiana sighed. It wasn't entirely Naveen's fault that he was a spoiled prince. Feeling a bit sorry for him, she began to teach him how to mince.

Soon Naveen was slicing the mushrooms all by himself.

By the time the meal was done, Naveen was feeling quite proud of himself. He had helped Tiana create something that brought their friends together for a good time.

Maybe there is some hope for this pampered prince, Tiana thought. Naveen finally seemed to see the value of good, hard work.

"There she is!" Ray cried, looking up at the night sky. "The sweetest firefly in all creation!"

Evangeline was really the Evening Star! Louis began to play his trumpet, and Naveen asked Tiana to dance. As they twirled under Ray's light, Tiana realized that she had learned something from the prince, too. Maybe a little bit of fun and romance wasn't so bad after all.

Tangled

A Dazzling Day

Adapted by Devin Ann Wooster
Illustrated by Brittney Lee
Designed by Stuart Smith

Long ago and far away, there lived a beautiful young woman named Rapunzel. She had a special gift: seventy feet of magical hair. She had never, ever been outside the tower where Mother Gothel kept her hidden away.

Every year on her birthday, Rapunzel gazed out her tower window at the sparkling lights that rose into the nighttime sky. The lights were meant for her—she was certain of it. And Rapunzel yearned to leave the tower, just once, to see those sparkling lights....

On the day before her eighteenth birthday, Rapunzel was wondering how to find the source of the lights. Suddenly, a thief named Flynn climbed into her window. Flynn was trying to escape from the royal guard, who were determined to catch him.

Pascal, Rapunzel's chameleon friend, agreed that Flynn did not look like the ruffians Mother Gothel had warned her about. So Rapunzel asked Flynn to guide her to the floating lights. Flynn agreed!

The next day, Rapunzel's heart fluttered as they neared the kingdom where the lights would be launched that night. She was so close—until Maximus, a horse from the royal guard, appeared. Maximus had finally hunted Flynn down and wanted to put him in jail. But Rapunzel convinced him to let Flynn go for just one day.

Just then, a lovely chiming sound floated through the air. . . .

57

Following the sound, Rapunzel raced up a small hill and saw the kingdom!

The chimes came from the kingdom's bells, ringing in the new day. Below the palace's peaked towers stood a village filled with thatched-roofed houses and inviting shops. Rapunzel felt more excited than ever.

Rapunzel was amazed by everything she saw in the village. People were talking happily, hanging out their laundry, and selling and buying things. They were all preparing for that night's launching of the

floating lanterns.

Rapunzel gasped in delight as she rushed to see more, but something *pulled* her hair.

People were accidentally stepping on all **seventy feet** of it!

Some little girls were braiding one another's hair nearby. When they saw Rapunzel approaching, their eyes lit up with delight. They had never braided such long hair before! When they were finished, Rapunzel walked away with a neat braid bundled down her back.

63

Nothing could stop Rapunzel now! She just had to wait until nightfall for the lights to appear. In the meantime, she found lots of new things to do in the kingdom! In a village shop, she tried on a beautiful dress.

Rapunzel shared pretty pink pastries with Flynn. She loved the way the sweet frosting glazed her lips and tickled her taste buds. She had never eaten anything this **marvelous** in her entire life.

Rapunzel found a bookstore and explored every shelf. She

pulled books down

to the floor and studied them with Flynn. She eagerly read adventure stories and saw pictures of foreign lands—all sorts of things she had never known about.

Rapunzel found people who were drawing beautiful, colorful pictures on the streets. Happily, she joined right in. She liked **everyone** she met!

"It is time, good people! Gather around! Yes, yes! Gather around!" A town crier was calling out to everyone. "Today, we dance to celebrate our lost princess. It is a dance of hope, in which partners start together, separate, and return to one another—just as our princess will return to us one day."

But as the man spoke, Rapunzel found herself standing in front of a large mosaic of the King and the Queen holding their baby. Something stirred deep inside Rapunzel as her green eyes met the identical green eyes of the Princess in the painting. And the Queen—why, she looked so familiar that Rapunzel's jaw dropped.

It was like looking in a **mirror!**

Soon everyone began to dance. Rapunzel and Flynn looked at each other shyly. Then they grasped hands and joined in, staring only at each other as they came together and separated among the joyous crowd.

Rapunzel felt as if she had lived a lifetime in one dazzling day. It changed the way she looked at the world.

It was beautiful and

wonderful out here!

At last, nighttime arrived. Flynn led Rapunzel to a boat and rowed away from the shore.

"What if it's not everything I dreamed it would be?" she asked.

"It will be," Flynn reassured her.

Darkness fell, and Rapunzel gazed in awe as thousands of colorful lanterns rose into the sky. It was her grandest dream come true!

Flynn reached behind him and pulled out a surprise for Rapunzel: two lanterns! Together, they launched them high into the air. Rapunzel's heart soared as the lights floated into the sky. It was the perfect end to a dazzling day. And all she could do was wonder what fantastic new discoveries were yet to come. . . .